33 36 8 20 38 18   46

This Ladybird Book belongs to:

_____

_____

_____

_____

All children
have a great ambition …
to read by themselves.

Through traditional and popular stories, each title
in the **Read It Yourself** series introduces children to
the most commonly used words in the English
language (*Key Words*), plus additional words
necessary to tell the story.
The additional words appearing in this book are
listed below.

Cinderella, happy, prince, dress, shoes,
dance, fairy, godmother, pumpkin,
changes, golden, coach, mice, rat, lizards,
footmen, almost, midnight, try, fit, marry

Ladybird books are widely available, but in case of
difficulty may be ordered by post or telephone from:

Ladybird Books – Cash Sales Department
Littlegate Road Paignton Devon TQ3 3BE
Telephone 0803 554761

A catalogue record for this book is available
from the British Library

Published by Ladybird Books Ltd Loughborough Leicestershire UK
Ladybird Books Inc Auburn Maine 04210 USA

Cinderella

by Fran Hunia
illustrated by Brian Price Thomas

Cinderella is a good girl.

She has two ugly sisters.

Cinderella works and works
in the house.

Her ugly sisters will not help.

They are going to the ball.

The prince will be at the ball.
Cinderella can't go. She has
no ball dress or shoes.

She has to work
in the house.

Cinderella helps her ugly sisters to dress for the ball.

"The prince will like us," they say. "He will want to dance with us."

The sisters go off to the ball and Cinderella works on.

She is not happy.

She wants to go to the ball and see the prince.

Cinderella looks up.
There is her fairy godmother.

She says, "Do you want to go to the ball, Cinderella?"

"I can't go to the ball in this dress," says Cinderella.

"Let me help you," says the fairy godmother. "Go and get me a pumpkin."

Cinderella gets a big pumpkin and gives it to her fairy godmother.

The fairy godmother changes the pumpkin into a golden coach.

Then the fairy godmother says, "Go and get me some mice, please."

Cinderella gets some little mice.

"Here you are," she says.

Her fairy godmother changes all the mice into horses.

"I want a big rat, please," says the fairy godmother.

Cinderella gets her a rat.

The fairy godmother changes the rat into a coach man dressed in red.

"Go and get me two lizards, please," says the fairy godmother.

Cinderella gets two lizards.

The fairy godmother changes the lizards into two footmen.

Then the fairy godmother says,
"Now I will make you a dress
for the ball, Cinderella."

She changes Cinderella's
dress into a ball dress.

"Here are some shoes for you,
Cinderella," says
the fairy godmother.

"You can go to the ball
and see the prince.
But there is one thing
I want you to do.
Please be home by midnight."

"Thank you, fairy godmother,"
says Cinderella.
"I will be home by midnight."

Cinderella gets into
the golden coach to go
to the ball.

Cinderella sees the prince
at the ball.

"Please dance with me,"
he says.

They dance and dance.

It's almost midnight.

"I have to go home," says Cinderella. She runs away. Her shoe comes off.

She runs on.
The coach and the horses are not there.
The coach man and the footmen are not there.

Cinderella has her working dress on.
She runs home.

The prince looks for Cinderella.

He can see the pumpkin,
the mice, the rat,
and the lizards.

But he can't see Cinderella.

Then the prince sees Cinderella's shoe.

"I will keep this shoe," he says, "and then I will look for her."

The prince looks and looks for Cinderella. All the girls try on the shoe but it will not fit.

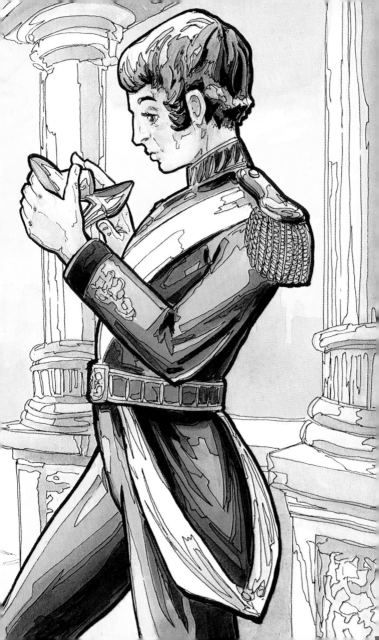

Then the prince comes
to Cinderella's house.

Cinderella's sisters try on
the shoe. It will not fit.

Cinderella says, "Please let me
try on the shoe."

"No, you can't," say
her sisters.

"Yes, you can," says the prince.

Cinderella puts on the shoe, and it fits.

The prince says, "Please will you marry me?"

Cinderella says, "Yes, I will marry you."

The fairy godmother comes.

She changes Cinderella's dress into a golden ball dress.

"Thank you, fairy godmother," says Cinderella.

Cinderella and the prince
get on the prince's horse
and away they go.

They are happy.

LADYBIRD
READING SCHEMES

Read It Yourself links with all Ladybird reading schemes and can be used with any other method of learning to read.

Say the Sounds

Ladybird's **Say the Sounds** graded reading scheme is a *phonics* scheme. It teaches children the sounds of individual letters and letter combinations, enabling them to tackle new words by building them up as a blend of smaller units.

There are 8 titles in this scheme:

1 **Rocket to the jungle**
2 **Frog and the lollipops**
3 **The go-cart race**
4 **Pirate's treasure**
5 **Humpty Dumpty and the robots**
6 **Flying saucer**
7 **Dinosaur rescue**
8 **The accident**

Support material available: Practice Books, Double Cassette pack, Flash Cards